This Little Tiger book belongs to:

Cameron

Christmas 2003.

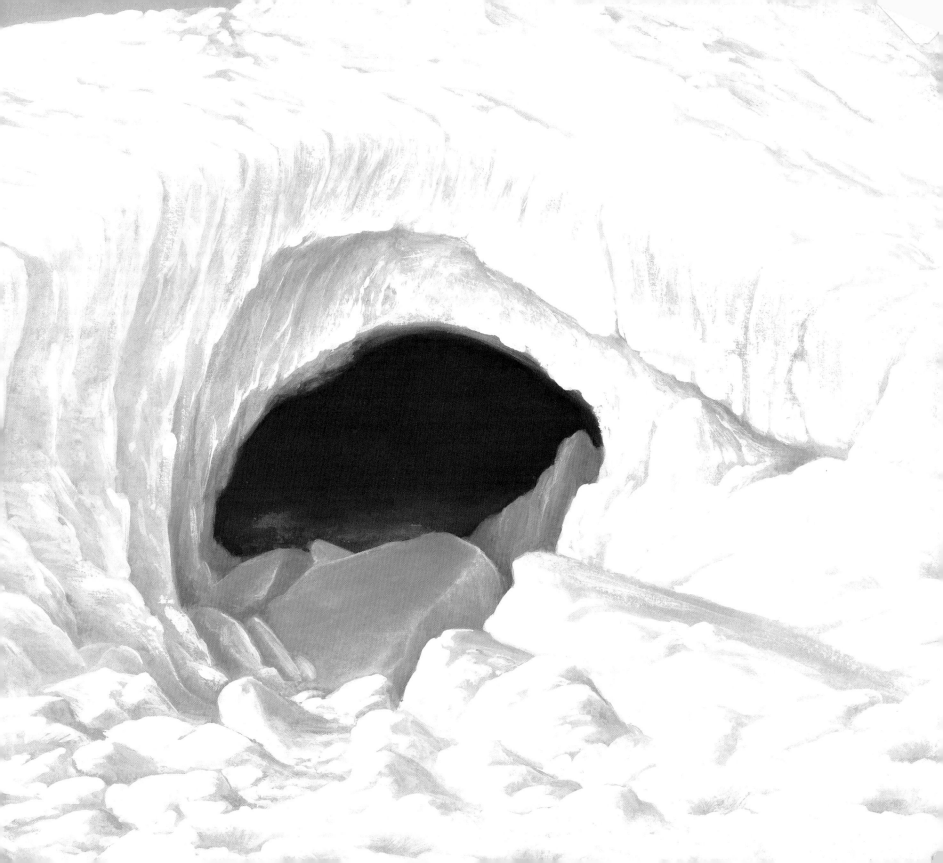

To Mum and Dad
JW

To my sisters ~ Dale, Glenis and Laura ~
with love and gratitude
NB

Foreword

Polar Bears are the most powerful beasts in the Arctic. They have survived there for thousands and thousands of years. Only Man could ever be more powerful than the bears. Recently Man has tried to tame the Arctic's frozen wilderness with modern technology, but the harsh, wild weather has defeated him. He has been forced to go, leaving behind strange objects that show where he has been. For the moment, Polar Bears have nothing to fear.

LITTLE TIGER PRESS
An imprint of Magi Publications
1 The Coda Centre, 189 Munster Road, London SW6 6AW
www.littletigerpress.com
First published in Great Britain 2003
This edition published 2003
Text copyright © Judy Waite 2003 • Illustrations copyright © Norma Burgin 2003
Judy Waite and Norma Burgin have asserted their rights to be identified as the author
and illustrator of this work under the Copyright, Designs and Patents Act, 1988
Printed in Singapore
All rights reserved • ISBN 1 85430 906 4
A CIP catalogue record for this book is available from the British Library

2 4 6 8 10 9 7 5 3 1

Nanuark

– a bear in the wilderness –

Judy Waite *illustrated by* **Norma Burgin**

LITTLE TIGER PRESS

London

High in the sky the last straggle of birds was flying south.

It was starting to snow. Soon everything would be hidden beneath the crisp, white layers.

Deep in this wilderness Nanuark's mother wanted to rest on their long journey to the sea.

While she was resting, Nanuark and his sisters found a place to play . . .

There were strange shapes and shadows. There were things that rolled and clattered and banged.

There were places with slopes to slip and slide.
There were places to climb and clamber and crawl.
"Beware of the Man Beast," the cubs called to each other,
scampering amongst a muddle of junk.

"It roars through the night with wild flashing eyes!"
shouted Nanuark's biggest sister.

"It tears down trees with its terrible paws,"
added the smaller one.

Nanuark crept up behind them both.
"And it GRABS little bears with its icicle claws,"
he roared, cuffing them playfully.

Their mother appeared.
"We must finish our journey,"
she growled softly, glancing
restlessly towards the horizon.
"We need to reach the Great
Water before the Big Freeze."

Nanuark dropped his head
sulkily. "Why can't we stay
here and play?" he grumbled.

"All polar bears head for the
Great Water this time of year.
We go to hunt for food, so
that we can survive through
the winter," his mother told
him. "Now keep close to me.
As close as a shadow."

Nanuark padded grumpily
behind her.

The snow thickened as it fell. Nanuark forgot to stay cross.
He jumped at the giant snowflakes, loving the tingle of cold
as the ice touched his tongue.

"Remember to keep as close as a shadow," his mother's deep
voice rumbled, as she called over her shoulder to him.

But Nanuark wasn't listening. He was too busy chasing the snow.

It fell faster, whirling round him in whispers of white.
Thoughts of the Man Beast drifted through his mind.
It prowled through his head, its wild eyes flashing,
its terrible paws tearing at trees, and its great icicle claws
reaching out to GRAB little bears.

"Mum!" called Nanuark. "Wait for me!"
But his mother was a long way ahead, and she didn't hear him.

Nanuark began to run after his mother, scrabbling in and out of her giant pawprints.

Suddenly he stopped.
He heard a scratching,
scraping sound.

A strange shape loomed
ahead in the swirling snow.
In the shadow of the shape,
something moved.

The Man Beast crept into
Nanuark's thoughts again.

*It roars through the night
with wild flashing eyes . . .*

But it wasn't the Man Beast.
It was a little ground squirrel.
He was searching through
a heap of rusty old metal,
looking for somewhere to
sleep.

Nanuark sniffed at the metal.
It seemed still and cold, as if
nothing had touched it for a
very long time.

He padded away.
If the squirrel wasn't scared
of it, then neither was he.

He ran on after his mother. The snow was covering her pawprints now.

The wind whined, whipping the snow into splinters of ice. Nanuark whined too.

Suddenly he stopped. He heard a snuffling, grunting sound.

A strange shape loomed ahead in the swirling snow. In the shadow of the shape, something moved.

The Man Beast slunk through Nanuark's thoughts again.

It tears down trees with its terrible paws . . .

But it wasn't the Man Beast.
It was a caribou, sheltering
beside a den made of wood.

Nanuark sniffed all round
the den. It seemed empty
and bare, as if nothing had
been in it for a very long
time.

He padded away.
If the caribou wasn't scared
of it, then neither was he.

Nanuark ran on after his mother, but her pawprints were gone. He called and called, but there was no answering growl.

The flicker of lights in the dark sky lit up a frozen land. Crystals glittered on the ground like angry stars. The wind screeched and skidded across the ice.

Suddenly he stopped. A strange shape loomed ahead. A new sound shuddered above the whistling wind. It was creaking and groaning. The Man Beast stormed through Nanuark's head.

It GRABS little bears
with its icicle claws . . .

Suddenly something lumbered towards him.

Nanuark ran forward with a whimpering cry. It was his mother!

"I've been so worried about you," she growled softly. "I thought you'd got lost. We've found somewhere to shelter while we wait for the Big Freeze. It groans and it moans, but it's only the ice shifting around it. I've sniffed through it carefully, and nothing has lived in it for a very long time. We'll make a den inside it and be safe."

Nanuark stared at the groaning, moaning hulk that lay locked in the ice.
"Is that the safe shelter?" he whispered. "I . . . I thought it was the Man Beast."
He pressed up close to his mother's soft warmth.

Nanuark's mother nuzzled his ears.
"The Man Beast is just an old Polar legend.
You hear all sorts of stories about it.
Some say they have found its scraps left behind in the snow.
Some say they have heard it calling from the bellies of great groaning fish.
Some even say it can fly. But I'm sure that even if a creature
as strange as the Man Beast did exist, it wouldn't stay here for long.
Not much can survive in this icy wilderness of ours."

Nanuark let his mother lick the snow away
from his eyes and his nose.

He gave a small growl of happiness. The Man Beast was probably just a story. And anyway, if his mother wasn't scared of it, then neither was he.

Keeping closer than a shadow, he followed her into the safe new shelter.

Free your imagination with books from Little Tiger Press

For information regarding any of the above titles
or for our catalogue, please contact us: Little Tiger Press,
1 The Coda Centre, 189 Munster Road, London SW6 6AW
Tel: 020 7385 6333   Fax: 020 7385 7333
E-mail: info@littletiger.co.uk
www.littletigerpress.com